Mojo and Weez
and the
Funny Thing

Written by Sean Taylor
Illustrated by Julian Mosedale

Collins

Mojo and Weeza found a funny thing.

Mojo said, "I know what it is!
It's a **boat**."

3

But the boat didn't float.

Weeza said, "I know what it is!
It's a **rocket**."

5

They counted ...10...9...8...7...6...5...4...3...2...1...
BLAST OFF!

But the rocket didn't take off.

Mojo said, "I know what it is! It's a **parachute**."

8

He climbed up a tree and jumped.
But the parachute didn't work.

Weeza said, "I know what it is!
It's a **tent**."
He lay down under it,
but the funny thing was too small.

10

Then it started raining and that was when
Mojo said, "I KNOW WHAT IT IS!"

Mojo turned the funny thing
around and it filled with rain.
Then he got in.
Mojo said, "It's a **bath**."

Weeza said, "Of course it is!"
And that's what the funny thing was …
well, sort of.

Storyboard

3

5

6

15

❧ Ideas for guided reading ❧

Learning objectives: Read familiar texts aloud with fluency and expression; relate story setting and incidents to own experience; use cues to check the meanings of unfamiliar words and make sense of what they read; become aware of dialogue, e.g. by role playing parts when reading; act out stories, using different voices for characters

Curriculum links: Science: sorting and using materials

High frequency words: off, take, that, what, would, then, are, up, a, tree, but, the, then, it, and, that, was, when, said, is, of, too,

Interest words: boat, rocket, parachute, tent, bath, umbrella

Word count: 147

Getting started

- Look at the front cover together. Introduce the characters Mojo and Weeza and ask children what they are looking at. Do Mojo and Weeza know what it is?

- Walk through the pages until p11, and ask children what is happening? What are Mojo and Weeza trying to do? (finding out what the funny thing is)

- Make a note of what the monkeys use the umbrella for on whiteboard: boat, rocket, parachute, etc. and read together.

- Read sentence 'I know what it is' and ask children if they can find it on other pages .

Reading and responding

- As the children to read independently and quietly from the start. Before starting, remind children to look at the pictures for clues for difficult words and use the whiteboard words for help.

- Ask them to practise direct speech in Mojo and Weeza voices.

- During reading, observe, prompt and praise each child in turn, for using grammar and punctuation to identify direct speech, reading in role' voices and modelling use of picture